To my grandsons,
Hunter and Conner,
who have given me
the joy of being a grandma...

and for Laurie, Kevin, Scott, David and the
rest of my family for their encouragement
in writing this story.
We all loved Heidi.

Her name was Heidi. She was beautiful. She was happy and full of life. She loved to run and play. She especially liked it when it was time to eat. When someone gave her a hug, she would wiggle and shiver all over.

She was a beauty with her long pointed nose and ears that stood up tall and strong. Her name was Heidi Von Bahem and she came from a long line of royalty — a real princess. And we loved our German Shepherd named Heidi. She brought us much joy and we brought her love and affection. She was our princess.

But it was not always that way. Her story was ugly. Heidi was born in a small town in Illinois. She was part of a litter of four puppies.

Their names were Heidi, Gretchen, Fritz, and Karla.

There is nothing cuter than German Shepherd puppies. They are black, and have floppy ears.

Their tan colors start to show on their plump little bodies as they grow.

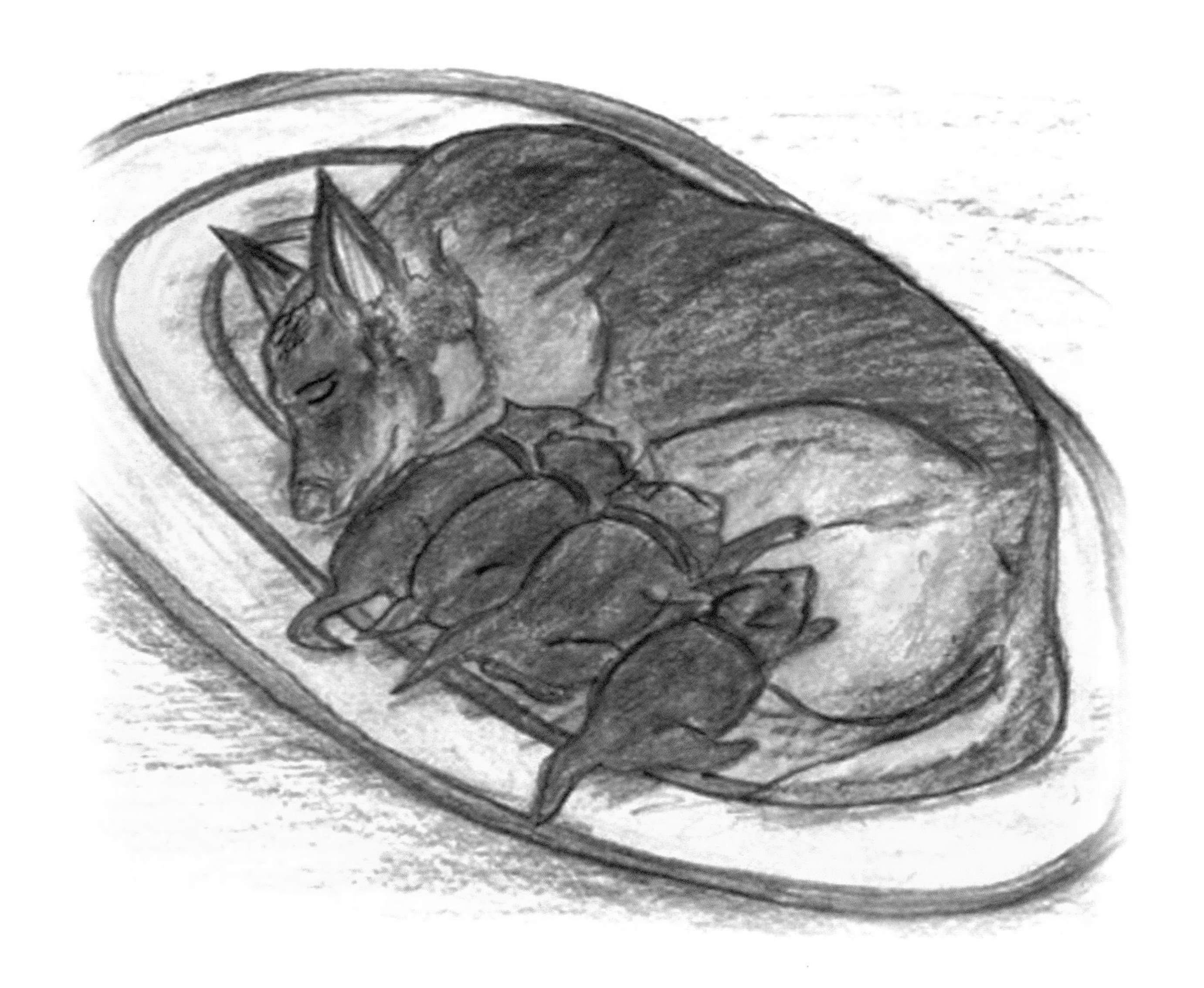

Heidi had a mother who took good care of her. She loved to snuggle against her mother and nurse along with the other puppies. For the first few days they would mostly eat and sleep. Their mother kept them full and clean with her tongue baths!

After a few days their eyes opened and they discovered that their short little legs would take them places. They also discovered that they could make noises with their voices. When the puppies were awake there was a lot of "yipping" going on. They were taken outside to play in the warm sunshine! They would wrestle and climb all over each other rolling in the grass. It was a happy time for Heidi. She would grow to be a friendly companion for some family.

By the time Heidi was three months old, she was sold to a family that lived in the big city of Chicago. They lived in a neighborhood where the houses are close to each other and dogs are often kept inside. They bought this German Shepherd to protect the family in this dangerous part of the city. They hoped that Heidi would bark and growl at strangers who came to their door.

The family was happy to have this new puppy. They would laugh at her as her little ears started to stand up. First one would stand up and then the other, then they would both fall down!

At first the children played with Heidi, but they soon tired of that. Heidi missed her brother and sisters. She was lonely. She would yip and yip, calling for just anyone to play with her. But no one came. Sometimes they forgot to feed her or fill her water dish. They did not keep her clean.

She was so lonely... and would cry out. She would sit on her back legs, and tip her head from one side to another trying to figure out why no one would play with her. She was lonely and she would yip and howl.

One day when Heidi was about six months old, the father came home from work very tired. He sat down to read the paper, and Heidi thought, maybe, just maybe, he would play with her so she started barking and running around.

As she ran past a little table, her wagging tail bumped a vase, and sent it crashing to the floor, all broken.

The father jumped up and shouted at Heidi, "I am sick and tired of your yipping and barking! You are a worthless no-good dog!" He opened the door to the basement, took his big booted foot and kicked her down the steps to the basement — bumping, bumping, bumping on each step until she landed at the bottom with a thud!!

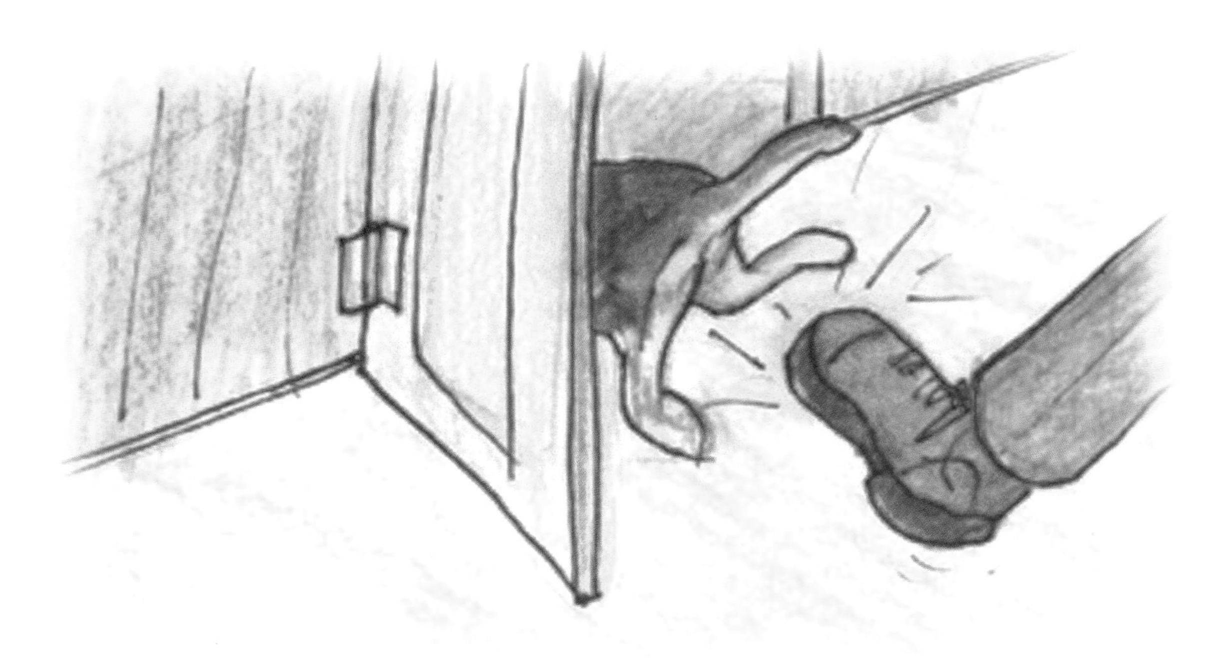

The sound that came from Heidi was not her playful yipping, but a sad little whimper... so sad. She could not move. Something was wrong. Her leg hurt terribly. And so she cried and whimpered in the dark basement all by herself.

They left her there all night, crying softly... all alone.

In the morning they discovered that Heidi had not moved all night, and that she could not stand up.

When they came down to check on her, she made a new sound — a low growl as she bared her teeth at them. They had taught her a new way — the way of cruelty, distrust and ugliness.

The father said, "Just what I need, a sick dog," and told his wife they had to take Heidi to the vet and see what was wrong. They put a leash on her, and dragged her up the steps. All the time she was moaning and growling to show them her anger and hurt.

When they got to the animal hospital, the vet said to them, "Why have you neglected this dog? What has happened to her? I will need to X-ray her leg."

He came out an hour later and said, "Her leg is broken. You will have to leave her here for a couple of days."

The father said, "Couple of days! I'm not paying for X-rays and two days at this animal hospital! You can have the dog. She is a worthless nuisance anyway."

And he walked out, slamming the door behind him.

For the next two days, Heidi was treated with loving care by the vet and his helpers. But she did not trust anyone anymore. They bathed her, fed her, and tried to stroke her with loving hands, but she only growled and bared her teeth.

The vet called his friend, Joe, where Fritz, Karla, and Gretchen lived and said, "Joe, you have got to help me find a home for Heidi. She has been abused and treated cruelly. I had to put a metal pin in her leg to make it strong. She'll make someone a great dog!" And Joe said he would see what he could do. He thought he knew just the place for Heidi.

And now this is not only Heidi's story, but mine as well.

My friend Joe called me one day and said, "How would you like a present?" I thought, "Well, who can resist a present?" So I said, "Come on over this weekend and show me my present!"

I waited anxiously for Saturday to come so I could see this present. When Joe drove in the yard, I was excited.

"Well, where is it?" I asked. "Where's my present?" Joe said, "Come here," walking to his van.

I looked in the back seat of his van and saw a pathetic dog, with ribs showing and sad, sad eyes.

I noticed then that it wasn't only ribs showing, but also bared teeth as the dog snarled at me.

Joe looked at me with a sheepish grin and said, "Sue, I want you to meet Heidi."

"Joe, Joe, Joe, what have you done to me?" was all I could say.

Well, we got a leash on Heidi and tied her to a post while we got a dog house cleaned up and ready for our new guest. I had to admit that our house in the country would be a great place for a dog to run and play and grow. But this sad, pathetic, dog who wouldn't even let me get close to her... I wasn't sure. I hoped I wasn't making a mistake.

I was a little nervous, in fact, a lot nervous, as I saw Joe drive away that day.

For the next few weeks, we tried everything we could think of to coax Heidi into being a happy dog. We wanted her to trust us. But she would lay stretched out with her head on her paws and growl every time we came near. We fed her by placing her food just inside the length of her chain.

We talked gently to her, trying to reassure her that she was home now and we loved her. But we only got snarls and growls. I wasn't sure we could ever get her to forget her time in Chicago when she was treated so cruelly.

And then, one day, Hallelujah!

We took food over to her and Heidi was standing up and wagging her tail. She was glad to see us. Maybe, just maybe, we could help Heidi become the happy, playful, loving dog she started out to be!!

The rest of Heidi's story is full of surprises and fun.

As she became more trusting, we were able to let her run without being tied up — run in the woods and pastures around our house.

In the spring she became friendly with the neighbor's Shepherd, Prince, and they mated. Nine weeks later it was time for her babies to be born. We watched her carefully, ready to assist her if she needed any help. We got up one morning to discover she was gone. We called and called, and could not find her. Finally, as we walked through the woods behind our house, we discovered a large fox hole, and heard noises in it. Heidi had gone into a foxhole to have her babies!

She ran in and out of the foxhole because she was so excited about her family! She was sharing the good news with her "people family."

We were worried that some harm might come to the puppies, so we coaxed Heidi out and my son crawled in and brought out six beautiful puppies! We took them up to the barn and made a warm spot for Heidi to take care of her babies. And what a good mother she was.

One time we let Heidi run, and after awhile we found she was missing. We looked north, south, east and west. We looked up and down, in and out. But no Heidi. She was gone. We were really sad thinking of her running and not knowing where her family was. We called neighbors and kept looking and calling.

After five days we had decided she had been shot or run over and we had lost her. Just then she came running up the driveway, wagging her tail.

She had been caught in a small barn at the neighbors when the door slammed shut — trapping her inside for five days! What a happy reunion that was for all of us!

We came to love Heidi more and more the longer she stayed with us. She had become part of the family. We were really sad to discover when she was 6 or 7 years old that she couldn't stand up. Her back legs seemed to be useless. The vet said that hip dysplasia is a common ailment of German Shepherds. Their hip joints become too weak and worn for them to stand.

I decided I would be Heidi's therapist! Since her front legs were strong, I put a big towel around her middle, held up her useless back legs and walked her around the yard several times a day. After a few weeks, she finally got better, and we could see her run in the woods and fields... happy with her life once again.

Heidi seemed to make up her own games. One day we were sitting out under the maple tree peeling peaches. She watched and watched as the curling peels would drop into the bucket below. Finally, she made a flying leap, caught the peeling before it hit the pail and went racing around us, as happy with herself as though she had caught a fly ball in a baseball game!

She was also a good catcher with food. Our family liked to roast sausage on the grill outside. She would sit patiently like a soldier at attention waiting for the cook to toss her bits of sausage hot from the grill. And she always caught them!

During the years that Heidi was with us, we also had two ponies, Sugar and Sandy. Heidi would crawl under the fence on her belly, commando style. Then she would stalk her prey. Only this time there was no intent to kill. She would get right up by them and start barking — enough to startle them, and off they would run with Heidi chasing them — all over the pasture! Her version of "tag."

Heidi was very protective of "her family" and her property. Shepherds are like this. They are very aggressive when it comes to their home and owners. She was like a sentinel watching at her post — taking care of us, and she protected us for many years.

Since we lived beside a wooded ravine, we often had “critters” come to visit us. If we watched the woods and fields we could see chipmunks, squirrels, rabbits, raccoons, opossums, deer, turkeys and groundhogs. We could even smell an occasional skunk. One summer we had a groundhog move into the barn, claiming the nearby garden as his own!

Even though these animals were a part of nature's family in our area, they were not welcomed by Heidi. This was HER place now, HER property, HER family, HER home and she did not welcome any strangers or intruders.

It is a natural instinct of German Shepherds to chase and kill small animals. Many times we saw Heidi relentlessly chasing rabbits or squirrels in the woods. Sometimes they were lucky enough to get away from her, but not often.

One day, as night was falling, we heard Heidi growling and barking out by her dog house. Something had decided to move into her house. HER HOUSE! NO WAY! So the attack began. Back and forth, in and out she fought, nipping and biting, trying to get the intruder out of her house.

Finally, with a vicious bite, she pulled that animal out of her house.

It was a badger — one of the most ferocious animals in our woods. But Heidi was the winner! No one was moving into her house!

When Heidi was about ten years old we found that her hip problem had returned. I tried for days on end to help her, using that old trick of the towel around her middle.

But her legs got weaker and weaker. Finally her front legs would not hold her up any longer. We made her a bed of straw in the barn, covered it with a soft blanket and gave her lots of loving care.

One day I noticed that she had some spots where the skin was wearing off her bones. I called the vet.

He looked at her and said, "I'm sorry, but that is not going to get better, only worse. It's time to let her go."

I sat down on the straw with Heidi's head on my lap telling her what a good girl she was and how glad we were that she had come to live with us, while the vet gave her a shot, and she just went to sleep.

In my mind's eye I can still see Heidi, running in the fields, coming home through the woods, jumping and playing, barking and yipping... in love with life.

Heidi was the first of many shepherds we were to have in the years to come. But there will never be another like Heidi. She was one of a kind...

A real princess.

Made in the USA